For Peter and Winnie
P.d.V.

For Griet and Rottie
P.G.

Carnival of the Animals

Philip de Vos and Piet Grobler

Front Street 8 Lemniscaat

**I**ntroduction

Come and join
the Carnival
with animals galore:
with beasts that crawl
or hop and skip
with a hee-haw and a roar.
Donkeys, lions, kangaroos,
hairy creatures found in zoos.
And added to this awesome list:
the dreaded beast –
the pianist!
And who will lead
this merry dance?
Our music man
Camille Saint-Saëns.

Lions

Lions will eat anything,
be it beggarman or king.
They love noses, they love toes.
They will eat you …
plus
your clothes.
But – don't give them
a brussels sprout –
and sauerkraut is also out.
Give them T-bones, give them meat,
but never, ever beans nor wheat.
I don't want one
as a pet myself.
For should it roar,
I'd wet myself.

 **hickens**

Chickens love to run around.
In the farmyard they are found.
But − dreadful is a chicken's fate,
when lying on a dinner plate −
minus
feathers,
minus
legs,
minus
cackle,
minus
eggs.
Life is really
not much fun
when one's parson's nose is gone.

**M** *ules*

It's a very mournful picture
when you're nothing
but a mixture
of a donkey
and a horse.
You get mixed up
and of course
your whole life
can get quite wonky
when you're neither
horse nor donkey.
It's not
so cool
to be
a mule.

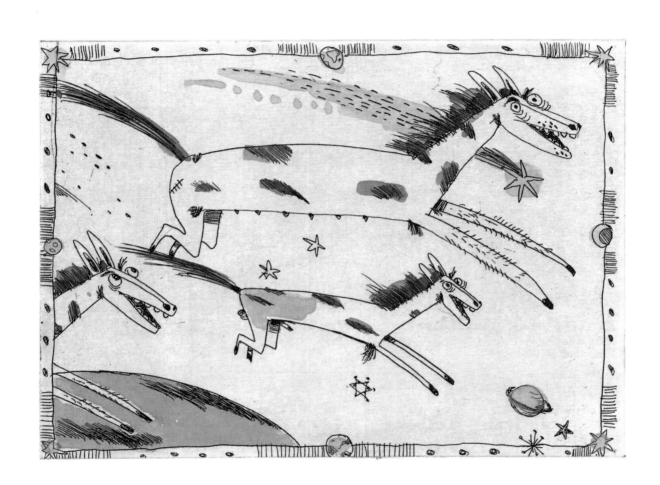

ortoise

Tortoise
cannot
sing or dance.
Tortoise
cannot leap or prance,
but
every night he does the can-can
like no woman, or a man can.
Then he waltzes, then he dances.
Then he hop-skip-jumps and prances,
till morning proves his dreams were wrong
and once again
he plods along.
He plods along, he plods along
until his tortoise days are gone.

Elephants

Elephants
have creasy skin
and lots and lots
of meat within.
They are fat
and they are jolly;
they are never melancholy.
They all scoff at eating rules.
They all love those kilojoules.
Their most hated word is
DIET
and they'll never, ever try it.
You'll be an unhappy chap
should one sit upon your
lap.

**K**angaroos

Kangaroos
sit
on their haunches
with their babies
in their paunches.

They hop and skip

in the Aussie sun.
You get
two
for the price
of one.

Aquarium

Fishes swim
without a goal
in aquarium or bowl.
We can watch them
through the glass:
bits of sunshine as they pass
in a circle round and round…
Little fish are nowhere bound.
They don't know
the mighty motion
of the waves and
of the ocean.
They must wait
for time to pass
locked up in a cage of glass …

onkeys

Consider now
the donkey's lot.
He'd love to be
what he is
not:
wild and lusty,
not so dusty,
with a song
that's not so
rusty.
Donkey
hasn't any choice
and mocks the world
with his
hee-haw voice.

# Cuckoos

Cuckoo birds are dreadful pests –
they lay their eggs in different nests.
They'll choose the home of a canary,
a dodo or a cassowary.
And though it seems a bit absurd –
cuckoos can fool any bird.
They love to jeer, they love to mock
when they invade a cuckoo clock.
I cannot rest
or sleep at all.
Please save me
from the cuckoo's call.
CUCKOO! CUCKOO!
Night and day.
How I wish they'd go away!

 *irds*

Birds of the sky, birds of the air —
scatter music everywhere:
sparrow, hoopoe, lark and jay;
birds that sing
to greet the day.
Turtledove
and crow and owl,
every single feathered fowl
twitter, tweet, tu-whit tu-whoo.
That is what all birds should do:
warble, chatter, squeak or cry.
Never ask the reason why.
Every bird
must have a song
and should sing it all life long.

Pianists

Many beasts
are in the zoo
and pianists
belong there too.
They are such a rowdy lot.
Playing till their fingers rot.
All those noisy honky-tonkers.
It's enough to drive you bonkers!
Every Tom
and Dick
and
Hannah
want to play the Grand Piannah.
Doh ray me fah soh lah te.
Please keep them away from me!

ossils

Please don't jostle
a poor fossil.
Fossils never snore in bed.
People say when you're a fossil
you are well and truly DEAD.
Still – those fossils
had their chance.
They could sing
and they could dance.
But – Tyrannosaurus-chorus
stopped a long, long time before us.
Life is short for man and beast,
so
while you can –
enjoy the feast!

*wans*

Swans
gaze
at
themselves
all
day
and never
have too much to say.
Swans don't cackle,
swans don't crow,
for there's one thing
swans all know:
Should they sing
just even one song –
that would be their final swan song.

inale

The Carnival of Animals
is coming to an end.
Perhaps you met an animal
that sounds just like a friend:
That pianist or donkey,
that person mad and wonky.
That one who cannot sing or dance.
That one who cannot leap or prance.
That friend who is too big and fat –
and with his weight can squash you flat.
That friend who now is dead and gone,
but had his turn like mule and swan.
Yes, man and beast all get a chance
exactly like
Camille Saint-Saëns.

Original etchings printed at:
The Caversham Press, Balgowan, KwaZulu-Natal